# We Der Superior World War II

## One person's thinking that led to destruction

Manish Chadda

NOTION PRESS

NOTION PRESS

India. Singapore. Malaysia.

ISBN: 9798891332164

*Dedicated to Civilians and Soldiers who sacrifice their
lives for or without the cause of War.*

**Disclaimer**: This book consists of a compilation of Adolf Hitler's writings, thoughts, and quotations from his books, accompanied by an analysis and explanations of his theories and actions. The biographical information regarding his life has been primarily sourced from Wikipedia. Please note that this book is intended for informational and educational purposes and does not endorse or promote the ideologies, actions, or beliefs of Adolf Hitler or the Nazi regime in any way. It is essential to approach this material with historical and academic scrutiny, understanding the profound moral and ethical concerns associated with the subject matter.

"Instruction in world history in the so-called high schools is even today in a very sorry condition. Few teachers understand that the study of history can never be to learn historical dates and events by heart and recite them by rote; that what matters is not whether the child knows exactly when this battle or that was fought, when a general was born, or even when a monarch (usually a very insignificant one) came into the crown of his forefathers. No, by the living God, this is very unimportant. To 'learn' history means to seek and find the forces which are the causes leading to those effects which we subsequently perccive as historical events."

— Adolf Hitler, Mein Kampf

# Prologue

Adolf Hitler's policies during his time as the leader of Nazi Germany had devastating consequences, resulting in the systematic persecution and murder of millions of innocent individuals, often on the grounds of their perceived racial, political, or social affiliations. Among the targeted groups, non-Jewish Polish civilians, Soviet prisoners of war, political opponents, homosexuals, the physically and mentally disabled, Jehovah's Witnesses, Adventists, and trade unionists suffered immense brutality and loss of life.

Non-Jewish Polish Civilians:

Hitler's aggressive expansionist policies and the invasion of Poland in September 1939 marked the beginning of World War II. As part of the Nazi occupation, Hitler's forces engaged in widespread violence against Polish civilians. The Nazis viewed Poles as racially inferior and subjected them to forced labor, deportations, and mass executions. By the end of the war, nearly two million non-Jewish Polish civilians had perished, a significant number of whom were targeted during mass shootings and in concentration camps.

Soviet Prisoners of War:

During Operation Barbarossa, the invasion of the Soviet Union in June 1941, Hitler's forces captured over three million Soviet prisoners of war. The treatment of these prisoners was inhumane, with many subjected to brutal conditions, inadequate food, and medical neglect. The vast majority of these prisoners did not survive their captivity, succumbing to disease, hunger, and violence.

Political Opponents:

Hitler's regime ruthlessly suppressed political opposition. Communists, socialists, liberals, and others who challenged Nazi ideology were arrested, detained, and often executed or sent to concentration camps. The Nazis silenced dissent and maintained their grip on power through terror and intimidation.

Homosexuals:

Homosexuals were also persecuted under Hitler's regime. The Nazis considered homosexuality a threat to the Aryan race and enforced draconian anti-gay laws. Thousands of gay individuals were arrested, subjected to forced labor, or incarcerated in concentration camps.

Physically and Mentally Disabled:

The Nazis implemented a disturbing euthanasia program, known as Aktion T4, and targeting individuals with physical and mental disabilities. Under this program, patients residing in institutions were systematically murdered, often through methods such as lethal injection or starvation. This program served as a precursor to the broader genocide that would become the Holocaust.

Jehovah's Witnesses, Adventists, and Trade Unionists:

Other groups, such as Jehovah's Witnesses, Seventh-day Adventists, and trade unionists, faced persecution due to their refusal to conform to Nazi ideologies or policies. They were arrested, imprisoned, and often subjected to forced labor or death in concentration camps.

It is essential to note that Hitler never publicly acknowledged or discussed the mass killings and the existence of concentration camps. His distance from the operational aspects of these atrocities was intentional, allowing him to maintain plausible deniability and evade responsibility.

The enormity of these crimes against humanity, along with the systematic murder of six million Jews during the Holocaust, paints a chilling picture of the ruthlessness and brutality of Hitler's regime. The horrors of this era serve as a stark reminder of the consequences of unchecked authoritarianism, intolerance, and discrimination. The memory of these atrocities continues to shape global efforts to prevent genocide and protect human rights.

# We Der Superior
# World War II

*"Soldiers and civilians, intensely propagandized by their government, usually carried their own caustic prejudices about their enemies, seeing them as brutish, subhuman beasts or fearsome 'Anglo-Saxon devils.' This racism, and the hatred and fear it fomented, served as an accelerator for the abuse of Allied prisoners."*

Laura Hillenbrand

Unbroken: A World War II Story of

Survival, Resilience and Redemption

Totalitarianism, Holocaust, Race, Superiority, Communism, Nazism, Adolf Hitler. Are these not seemed to be synonyms? You must be thinking there's something missing. It's World War-II. And, the all synonyms as I mentioned are the reasons of rise of Nazis and are catalyst for the World War-II. For some let's assume that World War-II was the after effect of World War-I, and that's the main reason. The Germans were penalized by the Treaty of Versaillies, which was signed in 1919 at the end of World War I, which imposed harsh penalties on Germany, including territorial losses, huge reparations payment, and restrictions on its military. Apart from that, what I see is, it's due to the complex that We the Germans, The Aryans are superior to any others, which Adolf Hitler had and led to the war which ended in 6 years in 1945, taken lives of lots of Human brutally. The Gas Chamber of Hitler, the Nuclear Bomb of Hiroshima-Nagasaki, Perls Harbour, and lot more to count.

Braunau am Inn, an Austria-Hungary town near the German Empire border in modern-day Austria, is where Adolf Hitler was born on April 20, 1889. The family relocated to Passau, Germany, when Hitler was three years old. Instead of Austrian German, the characteristic lower Bavarian accent he picked up there characterized his speaking for the rest of his life. In 1894, the family moved back to Austria and settled in Leonding. Alois retired to Hafeld, close to Lambach, where he farmed and kept bees, in June 1895. Hitler attended Fischlham's Volksschule, a public elementary school.

Hitler's failure to follow the severe rules of his school coincided with the relocation to Hafeld with, the start of intense father-son arguments. Despite his mother's best efforts to shield him, his father battered him. After Alois Hitler's farming endeavors in Hafeld were unsuccessful, the family relocated to Lambach in 1897. Hitler, then eight years old, studied singing, participated in the church choir, and even thought about becoming a priest. The family moved permanently back to Leonding in 1898.

Let's discuss about the aftereffect of Treaty of Versaillies, as mentioned earlier as signed at the end of World War I, which is one of the factor which trigger the World War II. What we understand it's a chain reaction, World War I - Treaty of Versaillies- World War II, then what....., How this treaty trigger the war? Let's try to understand that in few words that are, restriction, penalties, and sense of humiliation, economic hardship, and revolution. The restriction of any type and sense of humiliation are the main reasons for any revolution, some time internal as Naxalite movement or worldwide as outbreak of War.

The Treaty of Versailles, signed on June 28, 1919, marked the formal end of World War I and aimed to reshape the global geopolitical landscape. The treaty was a product of complex negotiations between the Allied Powers and Germany, seeking to address the causes and consequences of the devastating conflict. While intended to establish lasting peace and prevent future conflicts, the treaty's provisions and the manner in which it was imposed had profound and lasting aftereffects on international relations, diplomacy, and domestic politics.

The Key Points of Treaty Provisions were as. The treaty redrew the map of Europe, altering the borders of many countries. Germany lost significant territories, including Alsace-Lorraine, Saar Basin, and parts of Prussia. New nations emerged, such as Poland, Czechoslovakia, and Yugoslavia. Disputed regions like the

Sudetenland and Upper Silesia sparked ethnic tensions and territorial conflicts. To prevent future aggression, the treaty imposed strict military restrictions on Germany. Limitation of the German army to 100,000 troops. Prohibition of conscription, tanks, and aircraft. Demilitarization of the Rhineland as a buffer zone. The treaty placed sole responsibility for the war on Germany and Austria-Hungary. Article 231 ("war guilt clause") became a source of humiliation and resentment. Enormous reparations payments demanded from Germany caused economic hardships. The treaty established the League of Nations, an international organization aimed at preventing future conflicts. The League's structure, however, lacked effective enforcement mechanisms. The United States' failure to join and the absence of key powers weakened the League's influence.

The Treaty has had effects on International Relation. The heavy reparations burden and economic disruptions fueled hyperinflation in Germany. Social instability, unemployment, and poverty contributed to political turmoil. Economic hardships paved the way for extremist ideologies, including the rise of Adolf Hitler and the Nazi Party. The treaty's perceived injustices and territorial disputes continued to strain international relations. Italy's dissatisfaction with territorial gains led to tensions within the Axis Powers. Eastern European border disputes and minority rights issues sparked regional conflicts. The punitive nature of the treaty created resentment and a desire for revenge among defeated nations. Nationalist sentiments and a sense of humiliation fueled a desire to overturn the treaty's terms. The Treaty of Versailles failed to address underlying political, economic, and social issues that would later contribute to World War II.

Apart from the effect on International relations, it impacted domestic politics too. The harsh terms of the treaty provided fertile ground for radical ideologies to gain traction. Adolf Hitler's exploitation of nationalist grievances and anti-Semitic sentiments. The destabilization of Germany's political landscape enabled the

Nazi Party's ascent to power. The treaty's terms were widely criticized and deemed unjust by many nations. In Germany, the "stab-in-the-back" myth blamed politicians for the nation's defeat. The treaty's legacy shaped public opinion and influenced domestic policies.

To understand The Treaty of Versailles and World War II, let's discuss World War I. World War I, often referred to as the Great War, was a global conflict that lasted from 1914 to 1918. It involved many factors and complex interplay of events that led to its outbreak. World War I was a complex event with many causes. The late 19th and early 20th centuries saw a rise in militarism and nationalism in Europe. This led to an arms race and a growing sense of rivalry between the great powers. The late 19th century also saw a wave of imperialism, as European powers competed for control of colonies around the world. This led to tensions between the powers, as they vied for control of strategic resources and markets. In the years leading up to the war, the great powers had formed a series of alliances. This meant that if one power went to war, its allies would be obligated to join the war as well. This created a system of "entangling alliances" that made it more likely that a small conflict could escalate into a larger war. The assassination of Archduke Franz Ferdinand, heir to the Austro-Hungarian throne, was the spark that ignited the war. The assassination led to a series of events that culminated in the outbreak of war between Austria-Hungary and Serbia.

Other than these, there are some other factors that contributed to the outbreak of World War I. Like, The July Crisis of 1914, The Schlieffen Plan where a German military plan that called for a rapid invasion of France through Belgium. The plan was designed to defeat France quickly so that Germany could then focus on fighting Russia. And The British naval blockade of Germany was a major factor in the war. The blockade cut off Germany from essential supplies, such as food and raw materials. This helped to weaken the German war effort and contributed to the eventual Allied victory.

The outbreak of World War I was a major turning point in history. The war had a profound impact on the course of the 20th century, and it led to the deaths of millions of people. The war also led to the collapse of the Austro-Hungarian and Ottoman Empires, and it helped to create the conditions that led to the rise of Adolf Hitler and the Nazi Party.

Hitler, like many other Austrian Germans, started to form his nationalist views at a young age. He declared his allegiance to Germany alone, detesting the ailing Habsburg monarchy and its control over an ethnically diverse realm. Instead of singing the Austrian Imperial Anthem, Hitler and his companions used the salutation "Heil" and the German national anthem.

Hitler was forced to live a bohemian lifestyle in homeless shelters and a men's dorm in 1909 after running out of money. He worked as a casual worker and painted and sold watercolors of Vienna's landmarks to make money. Hitler was originally exposed to racist fashion in Vienna.

Adolf Hitler and the National Socialist German Workers' Party (Nazi Party) attempted a failed coup in Germany known as the Beer Hall Putsch, sometimes referred to as the Munich Putsch or Hitlerputsch. The Nazi Party drew inspiration from Italian Fascism in terms of their outward image and policy direction. Hitler aimed to replicate Benito Mussolini's successful "March on Rome" from 1922, envisioning a similar coup in Bavaria followed by a challenge to the government in Berlin. In pursuit of this goal, Hitler and General Erich Ludendorff sought the support of Gustav Ritter von Kahr, who held the position of Staatskommissar or State Commissioner and was effectively Bavaria's ruler. However, a crucial difference in their objectives emerged. Kahr, along with Police Chief Hans Ritter von Seisser and Reichswehr General Otto von Lossow, had their own plan in mind. They aspired to establish a nationalist dictatorship in Bavaria but were not necessarily in favor of Hitler's leadership. This difference in vision and ambition among these key figures in Bavaria's government created a significant tension and ultimately led to a complex and dramatic series of events in the early stages of Hitler's rise to power. On November 8 and 9, 1923, it happened in Munich, Bavaria. In the wake of World War I and the Treaty of Versailles, Germany was going through a period of political and economic upheaval. Hitler and his supporters thought they could topple the Weimar Republic government and install a new one led by the Nazi Party. Hitler and other key Nazi officials, including Ernst Röhm and Hermann Göring, stormed a meeting of the Bavarian government held in the Bürgerbräukeller, a beer hall in Munich, to start the coup. They proclaimed a national revolution and asked the in attendance government leaders for their assistance. The attempt, though, swiftly fell apart. The Nazis and the police engaged in a violent conflict after the government representatives at first resisted. Hitler and his supporters tried to march into the city center the next day, but they were met with armed resistance from the Bavarian government. Several Nazis were killed or hurt in the ensuing shootout on Munich's streets.

Hitler was able to flee the scene, but he was later taken into custody. In February 1924, he was put on trial for treason. Hitler garnered much media attention during his trial by using the courtroom as a forum to advance his nationalist and anti-Semitic beliefs. He was finally convicted of treason and given a five-year prison term, but he only completed a portion of it. In the short term, the Beer Hall Putsch itself was unsuccessful since it did not result in the toppling of the Weimar Republic government. But there were long-term repercussions. Hitler composed "Mein Kampf," an autobiographical manifesto explaining his political philosophy and objectives, while he was incarcerated. He attempted to revive the Nazi Party after being freed, and he used both legal and political measures to accomplish his goals. Hitler's ascent to power was significantly aided by the failed coup because it gave him national prominence and a forum to advance his extreme ideologies.

Hitler was influenced by his teacher and the fierce German nationalist Dr. Leonard Poetsch, who once said, "The great issue of the day will be decided not by means of speeches and majority revolutions, but by iron and blood." He was an Austrian-Hungarian. At that time, German speakers ruled a portion of Austria-Hungary. In Poetsch's view, Germany ought to be unified with these regions. So do Hitler.

And here came the well planned and designed attack of 31st August 1939. The Gleiwitz Incident. The Gleiwitz Incident, also known as the Gleiwitz Operation, was a staged false flag operation orchestrated by Nazi Germany on the night of August 31 to September 1, 1939, just hours before the German invasion of Poland. The incident was part of a series of coordinated events that provided a pretext for the invasion and marked the beginning of World War II.

The Gleiwitz Incident took place in the town of Gleiwitz (now Gliwice), which was then part of Germany but is now located in Poland. The operation involved Nazi SS operatives, led by Alfred Naujocks, dressed as Polish soldiers, attacking a German radio station located in Gleiwitz. The SS operatives were provided with Polish uniforms and equipment to create the illusion of a Polish assault.

At the radio station, the SS operatives broadcast an anti-German message in Polish and then reportedly shot dead a German-speaking prisoner from a local concentration camp. The staged attack was intended to be a provocation that could be used by the Nazi regime as a justification for the invasion of Poland. German officials later claimed that Polish forces had attacked the radio station and used the incident to support their narrative of Polish aggression.

The Gleiwitz Incident was one of several similar false flag operations carried out by Nazi Germany as part of what is known as Operation Himmler. These operations aimed to create a pretext for the invasion of Poland and to portray Poland as the aggressor, thereby providing Nazi Germany with a casus belli.

In the broader context, the Gleiwitz Incident was a small but significant part of the events leading up to World War II. It was used as propaganda to justify the invasion of Poland, which triggered the larger conflict between Germany and the Allied powers. The incident serves as a reminder of the manipulation of events and the use of propaganda for political and military purposes during this tumultuous period in history.

The Gleiwitz Incident serves as a cautionary tale about the dangers of propaganda, manipulation, and false pretenses that can lead to devastating consequences. The incident illustrates how governments or individuals can exploit fabricated events to justify military aggression and warfare. This incident highlights the power of propaganda and deception in shaping public opinion and justifying actions. It underscores the importance of critical thinking and skepticism when presented with information, especially in times of political tension. And also, demonstrates how a fabricated incident can be used as a pretext for military intervention or aggression. It reminds us to be wary of leaders who use false justifications to initiate conflicts, and the importance of seeking diplomatic solutions and peaceful negotiations to resolve disputes. Understanding the true nature of events like the Gleiwitz Incident encourages us to be aware of historical contexts and the manipulation of historical narratives. It emphasizes the need to study history critically to prevent the repetition of past mistakes. The incident raises ethical questions about the use of false flag operations and the manipulation of information to achieve political goals. It underscores the importance of ethical decision-making and accountability in leadership.

Overall, the Gleiwitz Incident reminds us to remain vigilant against manipulation, misinformation, and the potential for fabricated events to be used as instruments of war. It underscores the value of truth, transparency, and ethical leadership in preventing the escalation of international tensions and conflict.

Hitler originally came into contact with racial discourse in Vienna. Populists, like the mayor Karl Lueger, took advantage of the severe anti-Semitism in the country and occasionally promoted German nationalist ideas for political gain. In the Mariahilf neighborhood, where Hitler resided, German nationalism enjoyed a particularly strong support. Hitler drew heavily on Georg Ritter von Schönerer. He grew to respect Martin Luther as well. Hitler was a reader of regional publications like Deutsches Volksblatt, which stoked anti-Semitism and played on Christian anxieties about an inflow of Eastern European Jews. He perused the writings of thinkers and theorists, including Houston Stewart Chamberlain, Charles Darwin, Friedrich Nietzsche, Gustave Le Bon, and Arthur Schopenhauer in newspapers and pamphlets.

Hitler's anti-Semitism's genesis and evolution are still up for debate. Before he departed Linz, his friend August Kubizek alleged that Hitler was a "confirmed anti-Semite." Kubizek's assertion is, however, deemed "problematical" by historian Brigitte Hamann. Hitler claims in Mein Kampf that he first developed anti-Semitic views in Vienna, but Reinhold Hanisch, who assisted Hitler in selling his artwork, disputes this. Hitler interacted with Jews while he was a resident of Vienna."Historians now generally agree that his notorious, murderous anti-Semitism emerged well after Germany's defeat [in World War I], as a product of the paranoid "stab-in-the-back" explanation for the catastrophe," writes historian Richard J. Evans.

Adolf Hitler and the Nazi Party spread the false and virulent conspiracy theory that there was a "Jewish conspiracy" as part of their anti-Semitic propaganda. Nazi ideology was fundamentally anti-Semitic, and Hitler wrongly blamed Jews for a variety of social ills, such as Germany's economic difficulties, political unrest, and World War I military defeat. It is true that during World War I, German Jews showed their patriotism. Jews in Germany participated in the war in a variety of roles, including the military, like many other Germans did. In actuality, German Jews significantly aided the nation's war effort. Like their non-Jewish counterparts, they served in the army, navy, and other branches of the armed forces. Around

100,000 German Jews are thought to have enlisted in the German military during World War I, and they were frequently praised for their bravery and commitment. As you pointed out, a sizable proportion of Jewish soldiers perished in the trenches during the war. A false stereotype was that Jews were unpatriotic or disloyal. Hitler and the Nazis nevertheless persisted in spreading anti-Semitic conspiracy theories, blaming Jews for Germany's problems and campaigning for their removal and persecution notwithstanding the sacrifices made by German Jews to the nation throughout the war. The eventual adoption of discriminatory legislation, acts of violence, and finally the Holocaust during World War II were all significantly influenced by these incorrect views. It's crucial to keep in mind the devastating results of such irrational prejudice and discrimination, as well as the significance of eradicating anti-semitism and all other forms of prejudice.

Before discussing about the Supremacy, Racism and other Propaganda promoted by Nazi Minister Joseph Goebbels, here are some other key factors that contributed to the outbreak of World War II:

The Great Economic Depression of 1930, economic turmoil, which severely impacted many nations, leading to high unemployment rates, economic instability, and social unrest. These conditions contributed to the rise of extremist ideologies and nationalist movements in various countries. High unemployment rate means, high free educated persons, leads to in-personal economic instability, give rise to national movements may be sometime termed as anti-national. And what you say about the Expansionist Ambitions of Japan & Italy. Japan, under militaristic leadership, sought to expand its empire in East Asia, leading to invasion of China and other neighboring countries. Additionally, Italy, under Benito Mussolini, pursued territorial ambitions in Africa and the Mediterranean. Greed is the simple term for all these. There is a Sanskrit Sloka which says

*"Sanktani thadeva cha. Atilobhatvinshyti"*

*(Greed is the root cause of sin and all troubles, greed increases enmity; one who is greedier gets destroyed.)*

This greed somehow termed mildly as ambition, expansionist ambitions. Appeasement of some and expansionist ambitions of others and failure of the league of nations, established after World War I to promote international cooperation and prevent future conflict, proved ineffective in stopping the aggressive actions of expansionist power like Germany, Japan and Italy. In the face of Germany's aggressive actions, some Western democracies pursued a policy of appeasement (*A Hindi saying 'ek chup, sou sukh'* one silence, hundred happiness), attempting to avoid conflict by giving in to some of Hitler's demands. This approach only emboldened Hitler, who exploited these concessions to further his expansionist ambitions. This Ambitious and Determined person when become the Chancellor of Germany in the 1930s leads to Rise of Adolf Hitler and Nazi Germany. Soon after he start consolidating his power and establishing a totalitarian regime. The Nazis pursued expansionist policies, rearming the military and annexing neighboring territories, aiming to unite all German-speaking people under a single Reich.

There is a mix-n-match between ambition and ego. Ego is best described in Hindi is *'Ahankar'* or in this contest *'ahm'* that is 'I' 'I am, just I am.' In Simple Psychology, Ego is explained as "The ego is the only part of the conscious personality. It's what the person is aware of when they think about themselves and what they usually try to project towards others. The ego develops to mediate between the unrealistic id and the real external world." or "the self, particularly the conscious sense of self (Latin "I"). In its popular and quasi-technical sense, ego refers to all the psychological phenomena and processes that are related to the self and that comprise the individual's attitudes, values and concerns' as per APA Dictionary of Psychology.

Ego in Indian psychology: Ahamkara/ego, in both Yoga and Vedanta tradition of Indian psychology, is viewed as the surface self, which is mainly based on body and phenomenal experiences.

*Ahamkar bala darp kaam krodh ch sanshrita*

*Mamatmprdeheshu pradviksntoh bhasuyaka*

(A person who has ego, stubbornness, pride, lust and anger, these five vices are there. The God says - That person hates me with the Supreme Soul and looks at me with faulty eye. Everyone -This should be understood)

Hitler willingly volunteered in the Bavarian Army in August 1914 while residing in Munich and as World War I broke out. Hitler should have been sent back to Austria as an Austrian citizen, according to a 1924 report by the Bavarian authorities, therefore allowing him to serve was almost definitely an administrative mistake. He worked as a dispatch runner on the Western Front in France and Belgium while assigned to the Bavarian Reserve Infantry Regiment 16 (1st Company of the List Regiment), spending roughly half of his time at the regimental headquarters at Fournes-en-Weppes, which was far from the front lines. He participated in the First Battle of Ypres in 1914. The same year, he was awarded the Iron Cross, Second Class, for courage.

Hitler continued his artistic endeavors while working at headquarters, creating cartoons and illustrations for an army newspaper. He had a left thigh injury during the Battle of the Somme in October 1916 when a shell detonated in the dugout of the dispatch runners. Hitler recovered in a Beelitz hospital for over two months before rejoining his regiment on March 5, 1917.Both the 1917 Battle of Arras and the Battle of Passchendaele were witnessed by him. Hitler was given the Black Wound Badge on May 18, 1918, and in August 1918, he was recommended for and won the Iron Cross, First Class, a decoration that was uncommonly given to a member of Hitler's Gefreiter rank. He was hospitalized at Pasewalk on October 15, 1918, after suffering a mustard gas attack that partially blinded him. Hitler learnt of Germany's defeat while he was there and reportedly experienced a second bout of blindness as a result.

Hitler called the war "the greatest of all experiences" and received plaudits from his superiors for his valor. In addition to being outraged by Germany's capitulation in November 1918, his military experience had strengthened his German patriotism. His ideology started to take shape as a result of his resentment at the failure of the war effort. Like other German nationalists, he accepted the "stab-in-the-back myth" known as the Dolchstoßlegende, which held that although the German army was "undefeated in the field," it had been "stabbed in the back" at home by civilian authorities, Jews, Marxists, and those who signed the armistice that put an end to the fighting—later referred to as the "November criminals."

The initiation of World War I was a result of a complex interplay of events involving multiple countries and factors. It would not be accurate to attribute the entire responsibility for starting the war to a single party. However, the immediate trigger for the war was the assassination of Archduke Franz Ferdinand of Austria-

Hungary on June 28, 1914, in Sarajevo, Bosnia.

The assassination set off a chain reaction of diplomatic tensions and military mobilizations among the major European powers. Austria-Hungary, seeking to punish Serbia for alleged involvement in the assassination, issued an ultimatum to Serbia with demands that were intentionally difficult to accept. When Serbia's response did not fully meet Austria-Hungary's demands, Austria-Hungary declared war on Serbia on July 28, 1914.

The alliance systems in place further escalated the conflict. Russia, which had close ties with Serbia, began to mobilize its forces to support Serbia. Germany, as Austria-Hungary's ally, declared war on Russia on August 1, 1914. Germany then declared war on Russia's ally, France, and invaded Belgium as part of the Schlieffen Plan, leading to the involvement of the United Kingdom and other countries.

While the assassination of Archduke Franz Ferdinand was the immediate trigger, the underlying causes of World War I included factors like nationalism, imperialism, militarism, and alliance systems, as previously discussed. These complex dynamics and the decisions made by various nations contributed to the outbreak and escalation of the war. It's important to understand World War I as a result of a combination of factors and actions rather than attributing it solely to the initiative of one party.

Hitler went back to Munich after the First World War. He stayed in the army despite having no official schooling or future employment prospects. He was given the task of influencing other soldiers and infiltrating the German Workers' Party (DAP) when he was named Verbindungsmann (intelligence agent) of an Aufklärungskommando (reconnaissance unit) of the Reichswehr in July 1919. Party Chairman Anton Drexler was pleased by Hitler's oratory talents at a DAP meeting on September 12, 1919. He gave him a copy of his anti-Semitic, nationalist, anti-capitalist, and anti-

Marxist treatise My Political Awakening. Hitler applied to the party on the advice of his army superiors, and a week later he was approved as member 555 (the party started counting membership at 500 to give the appearance that they were a much larger party).

Adolf Hitler's rise to power in Germany in the early 1920s was characterized by the strategic recruitment of ex-soldiers and disenchanted individuals into a paramilitary force known as the "Brownshirts" or the Sturmabteilung (SA). These Brownshirts earned their nickname from the brown uniforms they wore, which were designed to evoke a sense of discipline and unity among their ranks. They quickly became a menacing presence in the Munich area, where the Nazi Party had its roots.

The Brownshirts operated as roving bands or small gangs, patrolling the streets with a clear intent to intimidate and exert control. One of their disturbing practices was to targeting Jews who crossed their paths, subjecting them to physical violence and harassment. This anti-

Semitic violence reflected the deeply ingrained anti-Jewish sentiments within the Nazi Party and foreshadowed the tragic events that would unfold in the years to come.

In addition to their street-level activities, the Brownshirts played a significant role in ensuring the security and dominance of the Nazi Party. They often attended Nazi Party meetings and rallies, acting as both security personnel and enforcers. When confronted with hecklers or political opponents, the Brownshirts did not hesitate to employ brutal tactics, wielding riding whips and hard rubber clubs to suppress dissent and stifle opposition.

This paramilitary force served as a vital tool for Hitler and the Nazi Party in consolidating their power and silencing opposition during a time of political turmoil and economic hardship in Germany. Their tactics of violence, intimidation, and suppression contributed to the erosion of democratic institutions and the eventual ascent of Adolf Hitler to the position of Chancellor in 1933, marking a dark chapter in German history and the lead-up to World War II.

Adolf Hitler's Brownshirts, or the SA (Sturmabteilung), were often deployed as a tool of intimidation and disruption in the early years of the Nazi Party's rise to power in Germany. One of the tactics they employed was to disrupt and intimidate rival political parties by attending their meetings or gatherings.

For example, if a rival political party, such as the Social Democrats or Communists, were hosting a public meeting or rally, Hitler might send a contingent of SA members to that event. Their presence alone would create a menacing atmosphere, as the Brownshirts were known for their paramilitary uniforms and aggressive demeanor. This could make the attendees and speakers at the rival party's event uneasy or even fearful.

Furthermore, the Brownshirts might engage in disruptive behavior, such as shouting down speakers, heckling, or starting quarrels within the audience. Their goal was to sow chaos, prevent the rival party from effectively communicating its message, and intimidate both the speakers and the attendees.

*"He is and remains a complete parasite, a scrounger, like a harmful bacteria always spreading further, (....) Has presence produces the effect of a parasitic plant. Wherever he settles, the people who welcome him will be wiped out eventually"*

*- Mein Kampf, Adolf Hitler*

In June of 1921, while Hitler and Eckart were engaged on a fundraising trip to Berlin, a rebellion erupted within the Nazi Party in Munich. Members of the party's executive committee expressed a desire to merge with the German Socialist Party (DSP) based in Nuremberg. Hitler returned to Munich on July 11 and, in a state of anger, submitted his resignation. The committee members soon realized that the departure of their prominent public figure and speaker would likely lead to the party's demise.

Recognizing the party's precarious situation, Hitler proposed his return on the condition that he replaces Drexler as the party's chairman and that the party's headquarters remain in Munich. The committee ultimately agreed to these terms, and Hitler officially rejoined the party on July 26, becoming member number 3,680. Despite his return, Hitler still faced opposition from some quarters within the Nazi Party. Those opposed to him in the leadership took action by expelling Hermann Esser from the party and producing 3,000 copies of a pamphlet that denounced Hitler as a traitor to the party.

In response, Hitler embarked on a strategic campaign, delivering impassioned speeches to packed audiences in defense of himself and Esser, earning thunderous applause. This strategy proved highly effective, and during a special party congress on July 29, Hitler was granted absolute authority as the party chairman, effectively replacing Drexler, with an overwhelming vote of 533 to 1.

The presence of the SA at rival party meetings often led to confrontations and physical altercations, further contributing to the atmosphere of political violence and instability in Weimar Germany. This tactic was part of the broader strategy employed by the Nazis to weaken their political opponents, undermine democratic processes, and ultimately pave the way for their rise to power.

According to Britannica, racism is, "Any action, practice, or belief that reflects the racial worldview—the ideology that humans are divided into separate and exclusive biological entities called "races," that there is a causal link between inherited physical traits and traits of personality, intellect, morality, and other cultural behavioral features, and that some "races" are innately superior to others. Racism was at the heart of North American slavery and the overseas colonization and empire-building activities of some western Europeans, especially in the 18th century. The idea of race was invented to magnify the differences between people of European origin in the U.S. and those of African descent whose ancestors had been brought against their will to function as slaves in the American South. By viewing Africans and their descendants as lesser human beings, the proponents of slavery attempted to justify and maintain this system of exploitation while at the same time portraying the U.S. as a bastion and champion of human freedom, with human rights, democratic institutions, unlimited opportunities, and equality. The contradiction between slavery and the ideology of human equality, accompanying a philosophy of human freedom and dignity, seemed to demand the dehumanization of those enslaved. By the 19th century, racism had matured and the idea spread around the world. Racism differs from ethnocentrism in that it is linked to physical and therefore immutable differences among people. Ethnic identity is acquired, and ethnic features are learned forms of behavior. Race, on the other hand, is a form of identity that is perceived as innate and unalterable. In the last half of the 20th century several conflicts around the world were interpreted in racial terms even though their origins were in the ethnic hostilities that have long characterized many human societies (e.g., Arabs and Jews, English and Irish). Racism reflects an acceptance of the deepest forms and degrees of divisiveness and carries the implication that differences among groups are so great that they cannot be transcended.

Hitler tended to defend his teaching with both religious dogma and evolutionary theory. He presents his discussion of racial purity on two different levels. First of all, every race save Aryans is essentially inferior. Second, because of their allegedly harmful traits, Jews, who are also often inferior, are held in much higher regard. Hitler asserts that genetic differences between the many kinds of life on Earth impose divides between them. He contends that going against nature is a surefire way to disaster and that the same principle of purity that forbids wolves from breeding with other wolves and loins from breeding with other loins also applies to human interactions. In the end, he contends that Jews will be accountable for nothing less than the eradication of the human race from the face of the world. His perception of superiority is based on comparisons between other races' levels of economic and cultural development. As a result, he saw the Japanese as being directly superior to the rest of Asia due to their greater level of economic growth in the area, which is probably why he allied with the Japanese during World War II.

*"If Nature does not wish that weaker individuals should mate with the stronger, she wishes even less that a superior race should intermingle with an inferior one; because in such a case all her efforts, throughout hundreds of thousands of years, to establish an evolutionary higher stage of being, may thus be rendered futile."*

*Mein Kampf, Adolf Hitler*

The claims of racial purity and superiority are central components of racist ideologies that have been historically used to justify discrimination, oppression, and even genocide. These claims are rooted in the false belief that certain races or ethnic groups are inherently superior to others based on their biological, cultural, or social characteristics. Such beliefs have had devastating and far-reaching consequences throughout history.

In the 19th and early 20th centuries, some scholars attempted to provide a pseudo-scientific basis for racial hierarchies. They made unfounded claims about the supposed superiority of certain races and the inferiority of others, often using biased interpretations of physical traits, such as skull measurements, to support their arguments.

The theory of Social Darwinism applied Charles Darwin's ideas of natural selection to human societies. It suggested that certain races or groups were more "fit" for survival and progress, while others were destined to decline. This theory was used to legitimize colonialism, imperialism, and racial exploitation.

The Nazis' distorted interpretation of the Aryan concept led to the belief in the superiority of the so-called "Aryan race." This belief formed the basis for their genocidal policies, including the Holocaust, which targeted Jews and other groups deemed racially inferior.

There were also limited opportunities for tranquility. Hitler argued that the Aryan race required 'lebensraum,' which is essentially the territory necessary for its growth and prosperity. He maintained that the supposedly superior Aryan race had both the entitlement and the obligation to acquire land from what they considered inferior races. Hitler did not conceal his brutal objectives; he openly aimed to invading Poland and the Soviet Union. Subsequently, he planned to forcibly remove or subjugate all Slavs and Jews while dispatching German settlers to occupy the newly conquered territories. This passage explains that Hitler believed the Aryan race needed more living space (lebensraum) to expand and thrive. He claimed that the superior Aryan race had the right, and even a duty, to take land from races he deemed inferior. Hitler openly stated his ruthless intentions to invade Poland and the Soviet Union, expel or enslave Slavs and Jews, and send Germans to colonize the conquered areas.

White supremacy is a form of racism that asserts the dominance and superiority of the white race over other racial groups. It has been used to justify slavery, segregation, and various forms of systemic discrimination against non-white populations.

Eugenics is the pseudo-scientific practice of controlling human reproduction to supposedly improve the genetic quality of the population. It often involved forced sterilizations and other coercive measures targeting marginalized groups, based on the false belief that certain traits were "undesirable."

Racial purity and superiority have been used to justify policies of racial segregation and discrimination in various societies, leading to unequal access to resources, opportunities, and rights for different racial and ethnic groups.

In the context of India, the term "Arya" appears in ancient texts such as the Rig-Veda, one of the oldest sacred texts of Hinduism. In these texts, "Arya" referred to people who were respected for their noble qualities and behavior, and it did not have the same connotations that were later attached to it.

You will find the trace of racism everywhere in all country and religion.

In Bhagvat Gita, Chapter 9, Verse 32, it says "All those who take refuge in Me, whatever their birth, race, gender or caste, even those whom society scorns, will attain the supreme destination.

*mama hi partha vyapashritya ye 'pi syuh papa-yonayah*

*Striyo vaishyas tatha shudras te 'pi yanti param gatim*

However, there persists a sense among some Germans of being superior and a source of pride in relation to notions of an Aryan pure race. Historical accounts mention instances where German women reportedly journeyed to the Ladakh town of Dahanu with the intention of conceiving, as part of an attempt to establish a lineage that they considered purely Aryan. The settlements of Dha, Hanu, Garkon, and Darchik are located on both banks along the Indus River, around 200 kilometers from Leh. The distinctive Buddhist Dard tribes, whose members are known as the Brokpas in the area, live in what is collectively referred to as the "Aryan Valley" in tourism circles. The Brokpas, who number fewer than 4,000 worldwide, have long been romanticized as the "last pure specimens" of the Aryan race due to their height and distinct physical characteristics (the blue irises).

Hitler addressed the Jewish question for the first time in writing in a letter to Adolf Gemlich dated September 16, 1919, which came to be known as the Gemlich letter. Hitler claims in the letter that the government's goal "must unshakably be the removal of the Jews altogether."

Hitler first met Dietrich Eckart, a founding member of the DAP and a practitioner of the esoteric Thule Society, there. Hitler was mentored by Eckart, who shared views with him and exposed him to a variety of Munich society. The DAP changed its name to the Nationalsozialistische Deutsche Arbeiterpartei (NSDAP, usually referred to as the "Nazi Party") in order to broaden its appeal. The party's logo, a swastika in a white circle on a red background, was created by Hitler.

Was the swastika not always associated with Nazism and hatred? The swastika is a religious emblem that originates in ancient Eurasia cultures and represents divinity and spirituality in Indian faiths. The swastika is a common icon found in both contemporary and historical objects, such as pieces of early Byzantine and Christian artwork, Mesopotamian relics, and art from the Indus Valley Civilization. Up until the 1930s, it was seen as a lucky and fortunate sign by western cultures. It became associated with anti-Semitism and racism in the 1930s when the Nazi party adopted it as a representation of the Aryan race identity. The Nazi party during World War II was the most significant organization to use the Swastika to represent nationalism and pride in pre-World War I Europe and thereafter. It became a representation of horror and anti-Semitism to Jews and other Nazi foes. Because of its connection to Nazism, the swastika is still seen as a sign of intimidation and racial dominance in many western nations today.

The Buddhist Swastika and Hitler's Cross: Rescuing a Symbol of Peace from the Forces of Hate (Stone Bridge Press, 2018) by T.K. Nakagaki claims that the swastika is one of the world's oldest and most ubiquitous symbols, dating back to prehistoric times. Dr. Nakagaki, an ordained Buddhist monk, makes a convincing case that the Nazi cross is not a swastika and did not originate from the customs that had elevated the Swastika to the status of a sacred symbol. Instead, the "hook-cross," also known as the Hakenkreuz, was Hitler's preferred cross. According to Webster's New Collegiate Dictionary, this cross was "used as the symbol of anti-Semitism or of Nazi Germany."

On March 31, 1920, Hitler received his military discharge and started working full-time for the party. Munich, a hot spot of anti-government German nationalists out to destroy Marxism and the Weimar Republic, served as the location of the party's headquarters. He addressed a throng of more than 6,000 people in February 1921, already a master of crowd control. Two truckloads of party members drove through Munich waving swastika flags and handing out flyer to promote the meeting. Hitler quickly became well-known for his raucous polemic speeches against the Treaty of Versailles, competing politicians, and particularly against Jews and Marxists.

Unfortunately, in the late 19th and early 20th centuries, the concept of Aryans was distorted and misused by some to support racist and supremacist ideologies. This led to the idea of a supposed "Aryan race" with claims of racial purity and superiority, which were later embraced and twisted by Adolf Hitler and the Nazi regime.

"Aryan originally denoted a group believed to have originated in ancient Iran and the northern Indian subcontinent, where they were thought to have spoken an ancient Indo-European language. The concept of an "Aryan race" emerged in the mid-19th century and persisted until the mid-20th century. This theory suggested that the probably light-skinned Aryans were the ones who migrated and conquered ancient India from the north. Their culture, literature, religion, and social structures were believed to have shaped Indian culture, particularly the Vedic religion that later evolved into Hinduism.

The notion of white racial superiority emerged in Europe during the 1850s, championed by figures like the Comte de Gobineau and later Houston Stewart Chamberlain, who coined the term "Aryan" to refer to the "white race." This so-called race was attributed to Indo-European languages, credited with human progress, and deemed superior to "Semites," Yellows and "Blacks." Among Aryan believers, Nordic and Germanic peoples were seen as the purest representatives of this "race." This idea was exploited by Adolf Hitler and the Nazis, despite being rejected by anthropologists by the mid-20th century, forming the basis for their genocidal actions against Jews, Roma, and other groups.

In the late 20th and early 21st centuries, various white nationalist groups incorporated the term "Aryan" into their names to promote their racist ideologies. Notable among these organizations were the Aryan Brotherhood, Aryan Nations (a hate group with Christian Identity roots), and the Aryan Circle, a significant presence within the San Quentin prison system. The term has since taken on a deeply negative connotation due to its association with racism, hate crimes, criminality, and Nazism.

The late 19th century in England witnessed a surge in hereditary thought. Influential figures like Francis Galton and Herbert Spencer propagated the idea of inherent racial superiority among the upper classes. Galton's works like "Hereditary Genius" (1869) highlighted how many of England's accomplished figures emerged from the upper strata of society. Spencer crafted a comprehensive framework merging biological evolution and societal progress, popularizing notions like rivalry, survival of the fittest, and societal prosperity. He argued against charitable efforts, labour regulations, women's rights, and education for marginalized and uncivilized populations. These ideas, collectively termed social Darwinism, aligned with prevailing racial ideologies ingrained in American culture, contributing to the adoption of IQ testing to measure innate aptitude and reinforcing notions of hereditary determinism across various facets of American society."

Adolf Hitler and the Nazi Party's rise to power was significantly facilitated by the high unemployment rate that developed in Germany after World War I. Extremist ideas and charismatic leaders flourished during this time of economic unrest and unemployment.

After the First World War, Germany was in a terrible state of disorder. Heavy reparations were placed on Germany by the Treaty of Versailles, which formally put an end to the war. This created economic instability and a severe depression. The democratic Weimar Republic, which was created after the war, strove to resolve the nation's economic problems.

In this environment, jobless rates increased to previously unheard-of heights. Millions of Germans were unemployed, which caused a great deal of dissatisfaction, desperation, and unhappiness among the general public. Families had difficulty making ends meet, and society as a whole felt bleak.

This ingrained discontent was noticed by charismatic and astute demagogue Adolf Hitler, who used it to his advantage. He appealed to the frustration of the unemployed and offered a way out through fervent speeches and propaganda. He appealed to nationalistic feelings and presented himself as the nation's rescuer in order to capitalize on the general desire for Germany to regain its previous greatness.

The radical nationalism, anti-Semitism, and authoritarianism of Hitler and the Nazi Party's platform resonated with a sizeable segment of the German public looking for a route out of their difficult conditions. Many people who had lost faith in the current political system responded favourably to the promises of job creation and the restoration of Germany's reputation.

Hitler started a number of public works initiatives as he ascended to power, including the building of the Autobahn, which appeared to deliver on his promises of job creation and economic recovery. While these programs did offer some respite, they also came at a high cost to democratic ideals and individual liberty as the Nazi regime tightened its hold on the country.

During and after Adolf Hitler's ascent to power, the Nazi Party provided a number of advantages to unemployed Germans. These payments were a part of a larger plan to win support and deal with Germany's high unemployment rate after World War I.

The Nazi Party first claimed to create jobs and revive the economy. The building of the Autobahn (highway system), which not only created employment opportunities for thousands but also improved infrastructure throughout the nation, was one of many public works initiatives started by Hitler's regime. Through their return to employment and the growth of the economy as a whole, this initiative attempted to lessen the suffering of the unemployed.

The Nazi dictatorship also adopted labour laws and steps to ensure job security. The establishment of the National Labour Service (Nationalsozialistischer Arbeitsdienst) and the Reich Labour Service (Reichsarbeitsdienst) forced jobless people to take part in public labour programs, assuring that they were actively contributing to the growth of the country. Even though these courses were frequently required, they gave jobless people a feeling of direction and organization.

Additionally, the Nazis provided unemployed people and their families with a range of social welfare services, including food and housing aid. This help was intended to lessen the financial problems faced by the unemployed, especially during the Great Depression.

The Nazi Party used methods other than economic ones to alleviate unemployment. Additionally, they encouraged a sense of patriotism and solidarity, which appealed to many unemployed Germans who felt demoralized and disappointed by the circumstances following World War I. Those who had lost hope benefited psychologically from Hitler's vision of returning Germany to its former grandeur and his ability to mobilize the populace around this objective.

In order to help the unemployed Germans, they provided social welfare aid, labour and job security initiatives, and projects that would create new jobs. Additionally, their emphasis on national pride and solidarity gave those who were struggling at a turbulent time in German history a feeling of purpose and optimism. The Nazi Party also sent general messages of hope and optimism to unemployed Germans in addition to these specific rewards. They appealed to the sense of national pride that many Germans felt and pledged to make Germany great once more. Numerous unemployed Germans who were eager for change were able to relate to this message.

The promises made by the Nazi Party to unemployed Germans were not as charitable as they first looked to be. It's critical to understand that these advantages were frequently a component of a bigger propaganda and control operation that had disastrous repercussions for Germany and the rest of the globe. In truth, the Nazis were mostly concerned in using the hardship of the unemployed as a political pawn to further their radical ideological goal. Adolf Hitler and the Nazi Party clearly rose to power as a result of the high unemployment rate in Germany after World War I, but it's important to recognize that their motivations were more influenced by political opportunism and manipulation than by real concern for the welfare of the unemployed.

After World War I and the ensuing economic instability, many Germans experienced widespread anger and despair, which Hitler and his party expertly exploited. They gained support from the public and consolidated their authority by promising to create jobs and boost the economy. They gained support from individuals who were in need of relief from unemployment and financial suffering by presenting themselves as the answer to Germany's economic problems. Once in power, the Nazis did carry out some job-creating programs and public works projects, such building the Autobahn, which did give some people jobs. To consolidate power, quell dissent, and advance their radical ideology, such as anti-Semitism and militarism, these actions were frequently subordinate to their broader objectives.

The unemployed were taken advantage of by the Nazis as a source of labour for their paramilitary groups and as a means of political intimidation. Young men were indoctrinated and militarized through initiatives like the Hitler Youth and the Reich Labour Service, and any who expressed their disapproval or resistance risked harsh repercussions.

In essence, Hitler and the Nazi Party were motivated more by a relentless quest of power and the imposition of their extreme ideology, even though the high unemployment rate in Germany was a crucial element in their rise. They used the suffering of the unemployed to advance their political goals, which ultimately led to the start of World War II and the destruction of much of the world.

*"All effective propaganda must restrict itself to a few key points and enforce them with stereotypical formulas as long as required until the lost of the audience is able to understand the idea"*

*- Mein Kampf, Adolf Hitler*

Hitler depended on his propaganda minister, Joseph Goebbels, to disseminate his message and shape public opinion. Goebbels utilized various methods, including the creation of posters with a powerful slogan urging Germans to unite in support of Hitler: "One People, One Country, One Führer." These posters, often accompanied by the Nazi swastika flag, were prominently displayed in public areas, ensuring widespread visibility and impact. Additionally, Goebbels introduced the phrase "Heil Hitler!" as the official Nazi greeting, further emphasizing loyalty and devotion to Hitler's leadership within the Nazi regime. These propaganda efforts played a crucial role in fostering a sense of unity and unwavering support for Hitler among the German population during the Nazi era.

Joseph Goebbels, Adolf Hitler's media adviser, and others were instrumental in formulating Nazi propaganda and spreading the Third Reich's ideology.

As the head of Nazi Germany, Adolf Hitler used propaganda as a potent instrument to further his political goals and keep the public under control. He employed mass media to spread notions of racial superiority, anti-Semitism, and Nazi ideology because he was aware of its persuasive power. Hitler was able to enthral and control the German populace because of his engaging speaking style and skilfully chosen imagery and symbols.

Hitler's top propagandist, Joseph Goebbels, sometimes known as the "Minister of Propaganda," was instrumental in directing the Nazi propaganda apparatus. Goebbels was an expert at influencing public opinion and fostering allegiance to the Nazi regime utilizing a variety of media, including newspapers, radio, movies, and public gatherings. He took advantage of contemporary communication methods to craft a tightly managed narrative that benefited the Nazi Party.

Hitler and Goebbels worked together to establish a widespread and deceptive propaganda machine that aimed to sway public opinion, garner support for Nazi programs, and advance the idea of Hitler as a charismatic and infallible leader. Their acts had a significant impact on the people of Germany, helping the Nazi ideology to propagate and the Holocaust's discriminating and eventually genocidal actions to be carried out.

Hitler was renowned for his captivating presence and impressive oratory abilities. He used large-scale rallies to enthrall and enliven crowds, frequently evoking strong feelings with theatrical gestures and passionate statements. These incidents demonstrated his capacity to appeal to the public and advance Nazi beliefs. Hitler's remarks at the yearly Nuremberg Rallies, where he spoke to hundreds of thousands of followers, serve as an illustration.

Joseph Goebbels understood how crucial it was to manage the media in order to influence public opinion. He oversaw the Nazi regime's takeover of newspapers, radio stations, and other media organizations, ensuring that only information deemed acceptable by the regime was broadcast. Nazi propaganda was intended to be disseminated to a large audience via the Volksempfänger (People's Receiver) radio. Through this channel, Goebbels spread messages of nationalism, anti-Semitism, and allegiance to Hitler.

The Nazis were adept at communicating their ideas through graphic means. Leni Riefenstahl's propaganda film "Triumph of the Will," which Goebbels influenced to be made in 1935, exalted the Nazi Party and depicted the Nuremberg Rally as a sign of cohesion and power. The impact of the Nazi propaganda was heightened by the careful cinematography and editing methods used in the movie.

To support their aims, Hitler and Goebbels constantly pushed anti-Semitic ideas. The Julius Streicher-edited publication "Der Stürmer," which had Goebbels' support, published derogatory depictions and erroneous stereotypes about Jews. This ongoing anti-Semitic propaganda effort aided in the growth of hatred and ultimately led to the Holocaust.

Hitler developed a personality cult thanks to Nazi propaganda. His persona was meticulously created to convey power, tenacity, and a sense of kinship toward the German people. Hitler was portrayed as a visionary leader who was leading Germany to glory in posters, movies, and pictures.

Nazi propaganda demonized and humanized those that were seen as the regime's opponents. For instance, advertisements and movies presented Jews as inferior beings who caused social issues. The systematic killing of millions was made possible by this dehumanization, which also prepared the path for discriminatory laws.

The goal of the Hitler Youth group was to propagate Nazi ideology among young Germans. Young people were taught to revere Hitler, embrace Aryan supremacy, and reject "inferior" races through camps, activities, and education. The goal of this propaganda campaign was to create a future generation of devoted Nazi followers.

The Origins of Totalitarianism examines European colonial imperialism from 1884 until the start of World War I, starting with the rise of anti-Semitism in central and Western Europe in the 1800s. Arendt examines the structures and practices of totalitarian movements, concentrating on the two real examples of totalitarian rule in modern history—Nazi Germany and Stalinist Russia—which she skilfully understands were two sides of the same coin rather than diametrically opposed ideologies of the Right and Left. She analyzes the transformation of classes into masses from this vantage point, the employment of propaganda to deal with the non-totalitarian environment, the use of terror, and the nature of isolation and loneliness as prerequisites for total dominance.

In Adolf Hitler's totalitarian ideology, there was no place for democracy. His brutal worldview, encapsulated in the Nazi Party's principles, rejected the core democratic principles of equality, individual rights, and representative government. Hitler firmly believed that governance should be the exclusive domain of an elite class, which he perceived as racially superior. According to his distorted vision, common citizens were meant to be subjects, not participants in the political process.

Hitler's disdain for democracy extended to his discriminatory policies. He advocated for the exclusion of individuals and groups he considered inferior, primarily Jews, Romani people, disabled individuals, and political dissidents. By denying them the right to vote, he sought to solidify the dominance of the Nazi regime and prevent any potential opposition or dissent.

This exclusion of certain segments of the population from the democratic process was a fundamental aspect of Nazi totalitarianism. It allowed Hitler to consolidate power without the constraints of checks and balances, judicial oversight, or public accountability. The suppression of democracy in Nazi Germany ultimately paved the way for widespread human rights abuses, the persecution of minority groups, and the horrific crimes of the Holocaust.

In sum, Hitler's rejection of democracy in favour of a totalitarian regime, coupled with his discriminatory policies, underscores the grave consequences of such ideologies when unchecked. It serves as a stark reminder of the importance of safeguarding democratic principles and protecting the rights and dignity of all citizens in any society.

Hannah Arendt's book "The Origins of Totalitarianism" is divided into three main sections. Anti-Semitism, Imperialism & Totalitarianism.

Anti-Semitism: Arendt explores the rise of anti-Semitism in central and Western Europe during the 19th century. She examines the historical and societal factors that contributed to the development of anti-Semitic sentiments and the subsequent persecution of Jewish communities. Anti-Semitism refers to prejudice, discrimination, and hostility directed against Jewish people based on their real or perceived Jewish heritage, culture, or religious beliefs. It has a long history that dates back centuries and has manifested in various forms, ranging from social exclusion and economic discrimination to violence and genocide. Throughout history, anti-Semitism has taken different forms and has been fueled by a combination of religious, social, economic, and political factors. It has often been used as a tool to scapegoat and blame Jewish communities for societal problems or to promote certain ideologies.

Imperialism: The book then shifts its focus to European colonial imperialism, particularly from 1884 to the outbreak of World War I. Arendt analyzes the expansion of colonial powers, the impact on indigenous populations, and how imperialism influenced the political landscape. Imperialism refers to a policy or practice by which a nation or state extends its power, influence, and control over other territories, usually through military force, economic dominance, or political maneuvering. This often involves the acquisition and governance of colonies or dependent Der territories, with the goal of exploiting their resources, labor, and markets for the benefit of the imperial power. Historically, imperialism has taken various forms, and different nations and empires have engaged in imperialistic activities at different times. Some well-known examples of imperial powers include the British Empire, which controlled vast territories across the globe, and the Spanish Empire, which had significant holdings in the Americas during the Age of Exploration. Imperialism has often been a source of conflict, exploitation, and resistance. Colonized or subjugated peoples often suffer from economic exploitation, cultural suppression, and loss of autonomy. The impact of imperialism has had lasting effects on both the imperial powers and the colonized regions, shaping political, social, and economic structures that continue to influence global dynamics. It's important to note that the practice of imperialism has been widely criticized for its negative consequences, including human rights abuses, cultural assimilation, and disruption of local societies. As a result, discussions about imperialism often involve debates about its motivations, effects, and ethical considerations.

Totalitarianism: In the final section, Arendt delves into the nature of totalitarianism itself. She examines how totalitarian movements, particularly Nazi Germany and Stalinist Russia, emerged and gained power. Arendt argues that these seemingly opposing ideologies shared fundamental characteristics and tactics, ultimately leading to similar outcomes of totalitarian control. Totalitarianism is a political concept that describes a system of government characterized by centralized and absolute control over all aspects of public and private life, often by a single ruling party or leader. In a totalitarian regime, the government seeks to exert complete dominance and influence over the economy, culture, education, media, and every other facet of society. Key features of totalitarianism include:

Authoritarian Rule: Totalitarian governments are highly authoritarian, where power is concentrated in the hands of a single individual or a small group. This concentration of power allows for swift decision-making and implementation of policies.

Ideological Control: Totalitarian regimes often rely on a dominant ideology or belief system that serves as a foundation for their authority. The state actively promotes this ideology through propaganda, censorship, and education.

State Control of Information: Totalitarian governments tightly control information and communication channels, manipulating or censoring the media, and using propaganda to shape public perception.

Suppression of Dissent: Opposition or dissenting views are not tolerated. Critics, political opponents, and potential threats to the regime are often suppressed through arrests, imprisonment, or even execution.

No Rule of Law: Totalitarian regimes may disregard the rule of law, using arbitrary or secret decisions to maintain control. Legal systems may be manipulated to serve the interests of the ruling elite.

Mass Surveillance: Citizens may be subject to extensive surveillance, monitoring, and censorship to prevent dissent or disobedience.

Economic Control: Totalitarian governments may exert substantial control over the economy, often employing centralized planning and directing resources to achieve specific goals.

Historical examples of totalitarian regimes include Nazi Germany under Adolf Hitler, the Soviet Union under Joseph Stalin, and North Korea under the Kim dynasty. These regimes exhibited extreme levels of control over their respective societies, resulting in widespread human rights abuses, suppression of individual freedoms, and in some cases, mass atrocities.

Totalitarianism stands in contrast to democratic systems, where power is distributed, and institutions are accountable, and individual rights and freedoms are protected. The concept of totalitarianism serves as a cautionary reminder of the dangers of unchecked power and the importance of upholding democratic principles and human rights.

Totalitarianism is a form of government characterized by centralized and absolute control over all aspects of public and private life, often involving an oppressive regime that suppresses dissent, limits individual freedoms, and exercises significant influence or control over the economy, culture, and society. While some proponents argue that totalitarianism can provide stability and efficiency, it also comes with significant drawbacks and dangers.

We can see there are few benefits of Totalitarianism as, Totalitarian regimes can impose strict control over society, leading to a sense of order and stability. This can be particularly appealing in times of social unrest or political turmoil. With power concentrated in the hands of a single authority or a small group, decision-making processes can be streamlined, potentially allowing for quicker responses to crises or emergencies. Totalitarian governments can exert significant control over economic activities, enabling them to implement centralized economic planning and prioritize national goals or projects. Totalitarian regimes often emphasize a sense of national unity and pride, which can foster a shared identity and a sense of purpose among citizens.

But apart from that, it's having list of cons too. Totalitarian governments frequently suppress individual freedoms, such as freedom of speech, assembly, and expression. Citizens' basic rights can be severely restricted, leading to oppression and a lack of personal autonomy. Concentration of power in the hands of a few individuals can result in unchecked authority and a lack of accountability, leading to potential abuse of power, corruption, and the absence of a system of checks and balances. Totalitarian regimes often use propaganda and state-controlled media to manipulate public opinion, shaping citizens' beliefs and limiting access to unbiased information. The focus on conformity and suppression of dissent can lead to social isolation and a lack of diversity of thought. This can hinder social progress, creativity, and the development of a dynamic and innovative society. History has shown that some of the most devastating atrocities, including genocide and mass persecution, have occurred under totalitarian regimes. While centralized economic control can lead to efficiency in certain areas, it can also stifle innovation and entrepreneurship due to limited competition and a lack of market-driven incentives. Totalitarian societies often prioritize the collective over individual needs and desires, potentially leading to a lack of personal fulfillment and a sense of meaning in life.

In summary, while totalitarianism may offer short-term stability and control, its negative impacts on individual freedoms, human rights, and social progress are significant and often far-reaching. The historical record of totalitarian regimes underscores the dangers associated with concentrating unchecked power in the hands of a few.

At the time of Hitler's release from prison, the political landscape in Germany had become less confrontational, and the economic situation had improved, which limited Hitler's opportunities for political agitation. Following the failed Beer Hall Putsch, the Nazi Party and its affiliated groups were banned in Bavaria. However, on January 4, 1925, during a meeting with the Prime Minister of Bavaria, Heinrich Held, Hitler made a commitment to respect the authority of the state and pledged to pursue political power through democratic means. This meeting paved the way for the ban on the Nazi Party to be lifted on February 16.

Despite these developments, Hitler's ability to engage in public speaking was restricted by the Bavarian authorities after he delivered an inflammatory speech on February 27, 1925. This ban on public speaking remained in place until 1927.

To further his political ambitions despite the speaking ban, Hitler appointed Gregor Strasser, Otto Strasser, and Joseph Goebbels to organize and expand the Nazi Party's presence in northern Germany. Gregor Strasser pursued a somewhat independent political course, emphasizing the socialist aspects of the party's program.

The situation changed dramatically with the stock market crash in the United States on October 24, 1929. This event had dire consequences in Germany, leading to widespread unemployment and the collapse of major banks. In response, Hitler and the Nazi Party seized the opportunity to gain support for their cause. They promised to repudiate the Versailles Treaty, revitalize the economy, and create job opportunities, tapping into the sense of crisis and discontent in the country.

On the night of February 27, 1933, a deep red glow appeared in the Berlin sky. Sparks and flames rose into the air. Berliners gathers in the street and watched a massive fire devour the Reichstag building, home of Germany's democratically elected parliament. The Reichstag, home of German parliament, goes up in flames. Hitler blamed the fire on the communists and used it as an excuse to turn German into a police state.

Under the pretext of countering the communist threat, Hitler initiated a harsh crackdown on all forms of opposition to Nazi rule. Immediately following the fire incident, he pressured President Hindenburg into issuing a decree known as the "Protection of the People and State." This decree had severe consequences for civil liberties in Germany, as it suspended freedom of speech and the right to gather in public. Government censorship of newspapers became permissible, and rival political parties were prohibited from organizing rallies. Anyone who dared to criticize the government could face imprisonment.

To enforce this decree, Hitler relied on his paramilitary force, the Brownshirts. These SA members conducted raids on communist offices and dismantled printing presses, effectively stifling opposition. As a result, approximately 25,000 individuals affiliated with communist and Social Democratic groups were arrested and detained.

On March 23, 1933, just a few months after the Reichstag fire incident, shortly after the Reichstag passed, Hitler convened a special session of the parliament and presented a crucial bill known as the Enabling Act which began the process of transforming the Weimar Republic into Nazi Germany, a one-party dictatorship based on the totalitarian and autocratic ideology of Nazism. This Act sought to grant Hitler the authority to temporarily suspend the constitution and make alterations to any existing laws. During the voting process within the Reichstag, a group of Brownshirts assembled in the hall and loudly chanted, "We want the bill... or we'll resort to violence and murder."

In the end, the Enabling Act was successfully passed into law, receiving a significant majority vote of 441 in favor and 94 against. This legislation marked a pivotal moment in the consolidation of power for Hitler and the Nazi Party, as it effectively allowed Hitler to make unilateral decisions without the need for parliamentary approval, further solidifying his authoritarian rule over Germany.

Fascism in Germany refers to the period of Nazi rule under Adolf Hitler's leadership from the early 1930s until the end of World War II in 1945. Hitler and the National Socialist German Workers' Party (Nazi Party) ascended to power through a combination of factors, including economic turmoil, political instability, and Hitler's charismatic leadership.

Hindenburg passed away on August 2, 1934, and Hitler took over as the nation's leader. In order to combat what he perceived as the unfairness of the post-World War I international system headed by Britain and France, Hitler sought to exterminate Jews from Germany and institute a New Order. The quick economic recovery from the Great Depression, the lifting of Germany's post-World War I constraints, and the annexation of regions inhabited by millions of ethnic Germans during his first six years in power helped Hitler win enormous popular support at first.

The Nazi regime under Adolf Hitler indeed embraced the deeply disturbing concept of racial hygiene, which was central to their ideology of Aryan supremacy. On September 15, 1935, Hitler presented two significant laws known as the Nuremberg Laws to the Reichstag, Germany's legislative body. These laws had grave consequences for various minority groups within Nazi Germany.

The Nuremberg Laws prohibited sexual relations and marriages between so-called

Aryans and Jews, and they were later extended to encompass other groups deemed undesirable by the Nazis, such as "Gypsies, Negroes or their bastard offspring." These laws not only enforced strict racial segregation but also stripped all non-Aryans of their German citizenship, effectively rendering them stateless and depriving them of basic civil rights.

Furthermore, the Nuremberg Laws imposed additional restrictions, including a prohibition on the employment of non-Jewish women under the age of 45 in Jewish households, further isolating and discriminating against Jewish families.

Adolf Hitler's eugenic policies also extended to individuals with physical and developmental disabilities. Under a program known as Action Brandt, which began in the early years of Hitler's regime, children with such disabilities were targeted. The program involved the involuntary euthanasia of these children, reflecting a horrifying disregard for human life.

As Nazi ideology grew more extreme, so did their actions. Hitler eventually authorized a broader euthanasia program for adults with serious mental and physical disabilities. This program, known as Aktion T4, aimed to eliminate individuals considered "life unworthy of life" through the systematic murder of those residing in institutions or care facilities. Aktion T4 served as a chilling precursor to the Holocaust and the mass murder of millions of individuals deemed undesirable by the Nazis.

The Nuremberg Laws, Action Brandt, and Aktion T4 illustrate the deeply disturbing and inhumane aspects of Nazi ideology, which led to the systematic persecution and extermination of countless innocent people based on their perceived racial or physical characteristics. These policies and actions are remembered as some of the darkest chapters in human history, serving as a stark reminder of the consequences of unchecked hatred and bigotry.

*If the international Jewish financiers in and outside Europe should succeed in plunging the nations once more into a world war, then the result will not be the*

*Bolshevisation of the earth, and thus the victory of Jewry, but the annihilation of the Jewish race in Europe!*

*—Adolf Hitler,*

*30 January 1939*

*Reichstag speech*

Hitler's quest for "living space," or Lebensraum, was a crucial ideological and strategic goal that significantly influenced his choices on foreign policy and was in fact a major factor in the outbreak of World War II in Europe. This expansionist ideology, which was motivated by ideas of racial superiority and the goal to create a Greater German Empire, attempted to secure land for the German people, particularly in Eastern Europe. Tensions increased as a result of Hitler's assertive foreign policy, which was marked by military buildup and territorial acquisition, and ultimately resulted in the start of the war. His attempts for rearmament were a flagrant breach of the Treaty of Versailles, which had severely curtailed Germany's military capabilities following World War I. This militarization further alarmed neighboring nations and contributed to a climate of fear and distrust in Europe.

Hitler gave the order to invade Poland on September 1, 1939, using blitzkrieg strategies, which involved simultaneous and overwhelming air and ground assaults. Due to the several international treaties that this act of aggression broke, Britain and France responded strongly and declared war on Germany. The start of World War II in Europe was formally signaled by the invasion of Poland. Hitler ordered the invasion of the Soviet Union in June 1941, violating the non-aggression agreement (Molotov-Ribbentrop Pact) that Germany had made with the Soviet Union in 1939. Operation Barbarossa, the invasion, aimed to destabilize the Soviet Union and seize control over vast eastern lands in order to advance Lebensraum's objectives.

Following the collapse of Poland, a conflict known as the "Phoney War" or Sitzkrieg (literally, "sitting war") broke out. Albert Forster of Reichsgau Danzig-West Prussia and Arthur Greiser of Reichsgau Wartheland, the two newly appointed

Gauleiters of north-western Poland, were given the order by Hitler to Germanize their regions with "no questions asked" on how this was done. Ethnic Poles in Forster's region were only required to sign documents attesting to their German ancestry. Greiser, on the other hand, concurred with Himmler and launched an ethnic cleansing operation against Poles. Greiser immediately expressed his displeasure that Forster was enabling tens of thousands of Poles to be recognized as "racial" Germans, endangering the "racial purity" of Germans. Hitler chose not to participate. This delay has been used as an illustration of the "working towards the Führer" thesis, according to which Hitler gave ambiguous orders and expected his followers to come up with policies on their own.

A policy of ethnic cleansing in Poland, supported by Heinrich Himmler and Arthur Greiser, called for the mass expulsion and eradication of specific communities, primarily Jews and Poles. This strategy was in line with Himmler's severe racial philosophy and his goal of forging a Greater German Empire that was racially unmixed. Hermann Göring and Hans Frank were on the opposing side of the argument. They supported a new strategy that aimed to use Poland's resources and agricultural potential to the Nazi government's advantage. The goal, according to Göring and Frank, was to use Polish labor and transform Poland into a "granary" or important source of food production for the Reich.

Initially, on February 12, 1940, the dispute was resolved in favor of Göring and Frank's viewpoint. This decision put an end to the economically disruptive mass expulsions at that time, in line with their strategy of utilizing Polish resources and labor. However, the situation evolved when, on May 15, 1940, Heinrich Himmler issued a memo titled "Some Thoughts on the Treatment of Alien Population in the East." In this memo, Himmler proposed the expulsion of the entire Jewish population of Europe to Africa and the reduction of the Polish population to a "leaderless class of laborers." Remarkably, Hitler endorsed Himmler's memo, considering it "good and correct." This effectively sidelined Göring and Frank's more pragmatic approach, leading to the implementation of the Himmler-Greiser policy in Poland.

On June 22, 1941, in direct violation of the Molotov-Ribbentrop Pact of 1939, a massive Axis force consisting of over three million troops launched a colossal offensive against the Soviet Union. Codenamed Operation Barbarossa, this invasion marked a significant turning point in World War II. Its objectives were multifaceted: firstly, it aimed to annihilate the Soviet Union as a political and military entity, with the intention of securing its vast natural resources for subsequent Nazi aggression against the Western powers. Secondly, it was an integral part of Hitler's overarching plan to acquire additional Lebensraum, or living space, for the German people. Furthermore, Hitler believed that a successful invasion of the Soviet Union would compel Britain to negotiate surrender, thus easing the pressure on the Western Front.

Operation Barbarossa proved staggeringly successful in its initial stages. Axis forces swiftly conquered an enormous expanse of territory, including the Baltic republics, Belarus, and West Ukraine. By early August, they had advanced an astonishing 500 kilometers (310 miles) into Soviet territory and achieved a significant victory at the Battle of Smolensk.

However, as the Axis forces approached Moscow, a critical decision by Hitler altered the course of the campaign. Against the advice of his generals, who had come within 400 kilometers (250 miles) of Moscow and believed that a direct push towards the Soviet capital was necessary, Hitler ordered Army Group Centre to temporarily halt its advance on Moscow. Instead, he diverted his powerful Panzer groups to assist in the encirclement of Leningrad (now Saint Petersburg) and Kiev.

This decision to change the strategic direction caused a crisis within the German military leadership. It provided the Red Army with a crucial window of opportunity to mobilize fresh reserves and regroup. Many historians, including Russel Stolfi, consider this pause to be one of the decisive factors that led to the failure of the subsequent Moscow offensive, which was eventually resumed in October 1941 and concluded disastrously for the German forces in December.

During this crisis and as a demonstration of his increasing interference in military matters, Hitler appointed himself as the head of the Oberkommando des Heeres, the High Command of the German Army. This move solidified his direct control over military decision-making, further concentrating power within the Nazi regime. The events surrounding Operation Barbarossa and its consequences had profound implications for the course of World War II, particularly in the Eastern Front, and marked a significant moment in the history of the conflict.

On December 7, 1941, a pivotal event occurred when Japan launched a devastating surprise attack on the American Pacific Fleet stationed at Pearl Harbor, Hawaii. This unprovoked attack prompted the United States to enter World War II, as President Franklin D. Roosevelt declared it a "date which will live in infamy." In response to this attack, the

U.S. declared war on Japan on December 8, 1941.

Four days later, on December 11, 1941, Adolf Hitler made a momentous decision. In a response that would further escalate the global conflict; he declared war against the United States. This declaration of war cemented the alignment of Nazi Germany with Japan's Axis powers and marked a significant turning point in the course of World War II.

Amid these monumental developments, another chilling and historically significant exchange took place. On December 18, 1941, Heinrich Himmler, one of the key figures in Nazi Germany and the head of the SS (Schutzstaffel), posed a question to Hitler: "What to do with the Jews of Russia?" To this inquiry, Hitler reportedly responded with the phrase "als Partisanen auszurotten," which can be translated as "exterminate them as partisans."

This statement by Hitler is deeply significant in the context of the Holocaust, as it is considered one of the closest pieces of evidence historians have to a definitive order from Hitler regarding the systematic genocide carried out during the Holocaust. The Holocaust, which entailed the systematic murder of six million Jews and millions of others, including Romani people, disabled individuals, and political dissidents, represents one of the most heinous and tragic events in human history.

Israeli historian Yehuda Bauer's commentary underscores the significance of this exchange and its implication in understanding the decision-making process behind the Holocaust. It serves as a haunting reminder of the extent of Hitler's involvement in the planning and execution of the genocide that took place during World War II.

By the end of 1941, German forces and the European Axis powers had indeed achieved significant territorial gains across Europe and North Africa. These conquests were part of the broader strategy to establish a vast German-controlled empire under Nazi rule. However, the tide of the war began to turn against the Axis powers after 1941, leading to a gradual reversal of these territorial gains.

While the Axis powers initially occupied vast territories, a combination of factors, including the determination and resilience of the Allied forces, the economic and industrial resources of the United States, and the internal weaknesses of the Axis powers, contributed to the gradual reversal of these gains. The defeat of Nazi Germany in May 1945 marked the end of World War II in Europe and the beginning of a new era of reconstruction and recovery for the continent.

In late 1942, a critical turning point in World War II occurred when German forces suffered a decisive defeat in the Second Battle of El Alamein. This defeat thwarted Hitler's ambitions to capture the Suez Canal and gain control over the Middle East. After earlier victories in 1940, Hitler had grown overconfident in his own military acumen, leading him to distrust his Army High Command and meddle extensively in military and tactical planning, which ultimately had detrimental consequences. One of the most catastrophic decisions came in December 1942 and January 1943 when Hitler repeatedly denied the withdrawal of the beleaguered German 6th Army at the Battle of Stalingrad, resulting in the near-total destruction of the force, with over 200,000 Axis soldiers killed and 235,000 taken prisoner. Subsequently, the Battle of Kursk marked another critical defeat for Germany, and Hitler's military judgment grew increasingly erratic. These strategic and tactical setbacks, along with Germany's worsening military and economic situation, mirrored the deterioration of Hitler's own health, contributing to the ultimate downfall of Nazi Germany in World War II.

In the midst of World War II, significant events unfolded in 1943 and 1944 that would further hasten the decline of Nazi Germany and its fascist allies:

Following the Allied invasion of Sicily in 1943, Benito Mussolini's grip on power began to crumble. After a vote of no confidence from the Grand Council of Fascism, Mussolini was removed from power, effectively ending his leadership of Italy. King Victor Emmanuel III played a pivotal role in this process. Marshal Pietro Badoglio assumed control of the Italian government and, shortly thereafter, made the momentous decision to surrender to the advancing Allied forces. This surrender marked a significant shift in the balance of power in Europe and the weakening of the Axis alliance.

Meanwhile, on the Eastern Front, the Soviet Union continued to exert immense pressure on Hitler's armies, pushing them into a steady and costly retreat. The resilience and determination of the Soviet Red Army played a crucial role in rolling back the German forces, leading to a series of significant victories for the Allies in Eastern Europe.

On June 6, 1944, a monumental moment in the war occurred with the commencement of Operation Overlord, the Allied invasion of northern France. This massive amphibious operation involved the landing of Western Allied armies, primarily American, British, and Canadian forces, on the beaches of Normandy. D-Day, as it is commonly known, marked one of the largest and most audacious military endeavors in history and opened up a new front in Western Europe.

As the Western Allies gained a foothold in France and continued their advance, many German officers and military leaders began to recognize the inevitability of defeat. They also became increasingly disillusioned with Hitler's leadership, which they saw as leading Germany toward complete destruction. This growing sentiment among German officers contributed to a series of conspiracies and attempts to remove Hitler from power in the later stages of the war, including the famous July 20, 1944, assassination attempt known as the "July Plot."

The combined effect of these events, including the fall of Mussolini's regime, the Soviet Union's relentless push on the Eastern Front, the successful Allied invasion of France, and the internal dissent within Germany's military leadership, all played pivotal roles in the eventual collapse of Nazi Germany and the conclusion of World War II in Europe.

In late 1944, the situation for Nazi Germany was becoming increasingly dire, as both the Red Army in the East and the Western Allies were advancing deeper into

German territory. Recognizing the formidable strength and determination of the Red Army, Adolf Hitler made a strategic decision to allocate his remaining mobile reserves against the American and British armies, which he perceived as weaker. On December 16, 1944, he launched the Ardennes Offensive, commonly known as the Battle of the Bulge, with the aim of sowing disunity among the Western Allies and, perhaps, persuading them to join the fight against the Soviet Union.

The Ardennes Offensive initially achieved some tactical successes and created a bulge in the Allied lines, but it ultimately failed to achieve its strategic objectives. The Western Allies rallied and pushed back the German forces, leading to the collapse of the offensive.

By January 1945, much of Germany lay in ruins, and the military situation was increasingly hopeless for the Nazi regime. Hitler, however, remained resolute in his defiance. He made a radio broadcast in which he declared, "However grave as the crisis may be at this moment, it will, despite everything, be mastered by our unalterable will," reflecting his unwavering determination.

As the military failures mounted and the Allied forces closed in, Hitler's view of Germany's fate became increasingly fatalistic. He believed that Germany had forfeited its right to survive as a nation due to its military defeats. In a drastic measure, he ordered the destruction of all German industrial infrastructures to prevent it from falling into Allied hands. The responsibility for executing this scorched earth policy fell to Minister for Armaments Albert Speer. However, in a courageous act of defiance against Hitler's destructive order, Speer secretly disobeyed it, preserving some of Germany's industrial capacity for post-war reconstruction.

Hitler's hopes of negotiating peace with the United States and Britain were buoyed by the death of U.S. President Franklin D. Roosevelt on April 12, 1945. He believed that Roosevelt's death might create divisions among the Allies and open the door to possible negotiations. However, contrary to Hitler's expectations, Roosevelt's passing did not lead to a rift among the Allied powers, as his successor, President Harry S. Truman, continued to cooperate closely with British Prime Minister Winston Churchill and Soviet Premier Joseph Stalin in their common goal of unconditional surrender from Nazi Germany. These events marked the final, desperate days of Hitler's regime and the inexorable march of the Allies toward victory in Europe.

Once in power, the Nazis established a totalitarian regime characterized by extreme nationalism, authoritarianism, and a fervent commitment to Aryan racial superiority. They swiftly dismantled democratic institutions, suppressed political opposition, and silenced dissent through propaganda and censorship.

One of the most horrific aspects of Nazi rule was the systematic persecution and mass murder of Jews and other minority groups in the Holocaust, resulting in the genocide of millions. Hitler's expansionist ambitions led to the outbreak of World

War II, as Germany sought to conquer and dominate neighboring countries.

The Nazi regime left a devastating legacy of war crimes and brutality, ultimately culminating in Germany's defeat and the Nuremberg Trials, where Nazi leaders were held accountable for their actions. Fascism in Germany serves as a stark reminder of the dangers of totalitarianism, xenophobia, and the erosion of democratic values, emphasizing the importance of safeguarding human rights and preventing the resurgence of such ideologies.

Hitler derided democracy as being essential and flawed, even on a national level, because it appealed to the view of the majority that he considered that to be an argument for the lowest common denominator and prevented people of real intellectual superiority and ability from taking positions of power. Hitler considered himself very much among the class of elite intellectual thinkers and evidence of his psychopathy can be seen dotted everywhere in his book Mein Kampf.

The advantage of widespread unemployment during the Great

Depression proved to be a critical factor in the rise of the Nazi Party in Germany. In the early 1930s, Germany was grappling with a devastating economic crisis. Millions of Germans were without jobs, struggling to feed their families, and losing faith in the political institutions of the Weimar Republic. It was within this climate of desperation and disillusionment that the Nazis found their opening.

Adolf Hitler and the Nazi Party astutely capitalized on this economic despair by presenting themselves as the solution to Germany's problems. They promised a swift and robust recovery, pledging to tackle unemployment head-on. Hitler's charisma and powerful oratory skills allowed him to connect with the suffering masses, offering them a glimmer of hope in otherwise dire circumstances. The Nazis promised to stimulate the economy, create jobs, and restore the nation to its former glory.

Furthermore, the Nazis leveraged the economic crisis to propagate their extreme nationalist and xenophobic ideologies. They played on the German people's sense of national humiliation stemming from their defeat in World War I and the harsh conditions imposed by the Treaty of Versailles. By blaming various groups, such as Jews and communists, for Germany's woes, the Nazis not only provided a scapegoat but also fueled existing prejudices.

In addition to their ideological strategies, the Nazi Party employed paramilitary tactics through their SA (Brownshirts) to intimidate and silence political opponents. The use of violence and intimidation contributed to an atmosphere of fear, making it more difficult for other political parties to compete. The Nazis' violent actions further pushed the desperate populace toward them as a perceived solution to the chaos and uncertainty.

Ultimately, the advantage of widespread unemployment provided the Nazis with the perfect conditions for their rise to power. They combined promises of economic recovery with propaganda, nationalist fervor, and intimidation tactics to gain popular support. Hitler's appointment as Chancellor in 1933 marked the culmination of their efforts, and the Nazis would go on to establish a totalitarian regime that would have devastating consequences for Germany and the world.

Due to the fiery speeches of Hitler and flawed economic policies by the Weimar republic, people of Germany lost faith in democracy. Hitler mixed racism in Fascism and started advertising Nazism. He became chancellor of Germany and declared himself Führer. He declared Germans as a 'superior race', promoted the idea of expanding 'living space' and invaded Poland and Czechoslovakia.

*"Church and state should be separate, not only in form, but fact - religion and politics should not be mingled"*

*- Millard Fillmore.*

According to Gandhiji, *"Religion and politics cannot be separated because religions inspire man to become virtuous."* But does the politics ever be virtuous, righteous or sinless.

It is unclear whether Adolf Hitler was truly religious or simply held beliefs in a higher power because of the uncertainty surrounding the subject of his religiosity. Hitler constantly refers to God throughout his speeches and views religion and the Church as essential components of the social structure he holds in the highest regard. It's interesting that he even goes so far as to say that the Church is more important than the State. Although his allusions to religious symbols and organizations might imply a connection to spirituality, further investigation is necessary to ascertain the exact nature of his beliefs.

According to Hitler, hatred cannot simply be sparked by a person's perception of their own superiority over another person. This idea has important ramifications since it suggests that rivalry is not always sparked by the idea of superiority alone. Instead, this feeling of superiority ought to compel one to believe that by natural advancement, they will eventually surpass the other and rise above them. Surprisingly, he views any attempt to purposefully harm the person who is viewed as being inferior as a futile exercise—a form of art distinguished by its futility.

Hitler frequently references the idea of God and weaves it into his story, which can be used to examine his religious leanings. He views faith and the Church as essential elements of the society structure and gives them a central place in the fabric of his beliefs. While this would imply a sincere spiritual bond, caution is advised because Hitler's use of religious rhetoric may have been motivated by political objectives. His deliberate use of religious motifs may have helped him to align his philosophy with socially acceptable standards or to instill a sense of moral justification for his deeds.

Hitler's claim that the Church is superior to the State also begs for investigation into the underlying logic behind such a declaration. This viewpoint clarifies his hierarchical worldview, in which religious organizations had a powerful position and may have even been used as a tactic to establish his authority. The nuances of his position, however, call for careful examination; was this sincere conviction or a cynical move to improve the social standing of his regime?

Hitler's idea that simple feelings of superiority are insufficient to produce hatred presents a provocative paradigm when one examines his thoughts on hatred. These emotions are thought to act as a motivator for human development rather than as a direct cause of hostility. This viewpoint is consistent with the idea that there is a natural evolution in which people compete with one another for advancement. As a result, assaulting individuals who are seen as inferior becomes a pointless exercise that prevents rather than promotes personal improvement.

Hitler's enigmatic religiosity highlights how complicated his personality and impulses were. It is unclear if his references to God and faith were genuine convictions or just ploys, despite the fact that they do indicate a certain degree of spiritual inclination. The Church being placed above the State in his hierarchy also makes one wonder about his true motivations. Additionally, his claim that hatred is not solely fueled by superiority offers a fresh look at how antagonism works. A fuller comprehension of these facets can help illuminate the complex web of Adolf Hitler's views and deeds as researchers work to piece together his diverse persona.

There are many similarities between modern dictators and historical characters like Hitler, both of whom constantly work to create "cults of personality" through influencing the media and society in order to appear as likeable and popular figures. This strategy, which is reminiscent of earlier occasions, is used to strengthen power and mold public opinion through carefully crafted narratives.

Hitler explores how his social ethics have changed; referencing his own observations of the suffering of Vienna's working class. He vividly depicts the depressing reality of a population that are unable to create prospects for advancement due to economic adversity. His story painstakingly analyzes the hand-to-mouth living, which alternates between scant food and famine, as well as homelessness, widespread alcohol misuse, and interpersonal discord. Hitler's vivid picture persuades us to believe that the circumstances he depicts were probably an accurate reflection of the time. It is impossible to dispute his prowess as a cunning manipulator and a brilliant storyteller.

From Hitler's perspective, the entire Jewish enterprise was being orchestrated toward a single, overarching goal: the tyranny of the entire human species. His doctrine is supported by a synthesis of evolutionary theory and religious values. His discussion of racial purity is divided into two parts. He declares that all races—aside from Aryans—are essentially inferior. Second, he places Jews in a position of even greater disgust because of their allegedly dangerous characteristics. Regarding genetics, Hitler argues that there are fundamental differences between different species in the biosphere. He asserts that the same rules of purity observed in the breeding of lions and wolves apply equally to human interactions, and that violating these natural distinctions invites inevitable disaster.

*"The Jews are undoubtedly a race, but they are not human."*

*— Adolf Hitler*

(He thinks himself that I'm the doer under the control of ego. An arrogant man is a foolish soul.)

"We are, what we are and there is no one superior to us". This was the thinking of Germans and of Japanese too.

*Maan sahit vish khae ke, sambhu bhaye jagdish*

*Bina maan amrit piye, rahu katayo sish*

(Lord Shankar drank poison to protect the whole world and, in spite of his He did not allow himself to be with ego or proud and thus became Jadish, The Lord of the whole World. On the other hand, the planet Rahu, after drinking nectar, was frantic in ego and had to cut off his head.)

There is a story from *Puranic* texts, about *Samundra Manthan , Mohini and Svarbhanu (Asura).* The tales begin in the "remotest periods of the earliest of time, when the devas and asuras churned the ocean of milk to extract from it the amrita, the elixir of immortality." Mohini, the female avatar of Vishnu, started distributing amrita to the devas. However, one of the asuras, Svarbhanu, sat in the row of devas and drank the amrita. Surya and Chandra noticed him and they informed Mohini; however, by that time, Svarbhanu had already become immortal. Vishnu, as Mohini, cut off Svarbhanu's head with his discus, the Sudarshana Chakra. Svarbhanu, henceforth referred to as Rahu and Ketu, could not die, but his head was separated from his body; his head came to be known as Rahu, while his body came to be known as Ketu. Following this event, Rahu and Ketu gained the status of planets, and could influence the lives of humans on Earth. Rahu and Ketu became bitter enemies with Surya (Sun) and Chandra (Moon) for exposing his deception and leading to his decapitation. For this, Rahu pursues them and attempts to consume the Sun and Moon. Since Rahu is the head without the body, the Sun and Moon exit from his throat when he tries to swallow them. This recurring cycle creates the grahana, an eclipse of the Sun and the Moon, which represents the temporary revenge of Rahu.

As in the 1930s, after Adolf Hitler became Chancellor of Germany, his ego led him to his tragic suicide via gunshots on 30 April 1945, as Soviet troops entered the heart of Berlin.

In the final days of World War II, Adolf Hitler's life took a dramatic and tragic turn. On the night of April 28-29, 1945, after midnight, Hitler and Eva Braun were married in a small civil ceremony within the confines of the Führerbunker, an underground bunker complex in Berlin where Hitler and his closest associates had taken refuge. This marriage was a clandestine and deeply personal event, reflecting the chaotic and desperate situation Germany found itself in during these closing moments of the war.

Later that afternoon, on April 29, 1945, Hitler received devastating news. He was informed that Benito Mussolini, the former leader of Italy and a key Axis ally, had been captured and executed by Italian partisans the previous day. Mussolini's death served as a stark reminder of the grim fate that could await leaders of the Axis powers if they fell into the hands of victorious Allied forces or resistance movements. This news likely heightened Hitler's determination to evade capture at all costs, as he faced the imminent collapse of Nazi Germany and the encroachment of Allied forces on Berlin.

In the following days, as the Soviet Red Army closed in on the Führerbunker and the end of the war approached, Hitler and Eva Braun remained in the bunker complex. Ultimately, on April 30, 1945, faced with the inescapable reality of defeat, Hitler took his own life by ingesting poison and shooting himself in the head. Eva Braun also ingested poison and died by his side. Their deaths marked the symbolic end of Nazi Germany and the closing chapter of World War II in Europe.

Conclusion:

The intertwining of the terms "Aryan" and "Hitler" was a crucial factor in the events leading up to and during World War II. Hitler's belief in Aryan supremacy and the alleged Aryan heritage of the Germanic people shaped Nazi ideology and contributed to the causes of the war. The Aryan myth, with its distorted historical connections, provided a flawed justification for racist policies and the horrors of the Holocaust.

Understanding the role of Aryan ideology in World War II serves as a solemn reminder of the dangers of racist ideologies taken to their extreme. It highlights the importance of promoting tolerance, inclusivity, and respect for all individuals, regardless of their race or ethnicity, to prevent the recurrence of such catastrophic events in the future

## WHY DOESN'T THIS WALL OF IGNORANCE BREAK?

# **Chronology of Aryan travel**

The timeline and details of Aryan migrations and invasions are subjects of ongoing research and scholarly debate. The concept of Aryan migration refers to the hypothetical movement of Indo-European-speaking groups into various regions, including the Indian subcontinent. However, it's important to note that the term "invasion" is often contested, and some scholars prefer terms like "migration" or "interaction" to describe these historical processes.

Here is a broad overview of the Aryan migrations and interactions in the Indian subcontinent, based on current scholarly understanding:

<u>Bronze Age and Early Vedic Period (approx. 2000 BCE - 1500 BCE):</u>

Indo-European-speaking groups, often referred to as Aryans, are believed to have been part of the broader Indo-Iranian cultural and linguistic group.

These groups are thought to have migrated from the northwestern regions (potentially from the Eurasian Steppe) into the northwestern parts of the Indian subcontinent.

The earliest hymns of the Rig-Veda, a collection of ancient Sanskrit hymns, are believed to have been composed during this period. The Rig-Veda provides insights into the religious and cultural aspects of these early Indo-Aryan societies.

Later Vedic Period (approx. 1500 BCE - 600 BCE):

Aryan societies continued to expand eastward and southward within the Indian subcontinent.

The later Vedic texts, such as the Yajurveda, Samaveda, and Atharvaveda, were composed during this period.

The Aryan societies engaged in interactions with existing non-Aryan cultures and peoples, leading to the development of a diverse cultural landscape.

Emergence of Early States and Kingdoms (approx. 600 BCE - 300 BCE):

Over time, Aryan societies contributed to the formation of early states and kingdoms in different regions of the Indian subcontinent.

<u>The Mauryan and Gupta empires (c. 4th century BCE - 6th century CE)</u> are examples of historical periods when various parts of the subcontinent were politically unified.

It's crucial to highlight that the movements and interactions of the Aryans were intricate and diverse, unfolding across an extended period. The term "Aryan" has undergone numerous interpretations and scholarly discussions, and contemporary comprehension recognizes the complexities and ambiguities linked to this term. It is essential to acknowledge that studying Aryan migrations and their impact involves navigating through various historical, linguistic, and archaeological sources while remaining aware of the interpretive challenges that arise from the multifaceted nature of these ancient movements.

# Timeline of World War II

1939:

January 30: Hitler declares German territorial demands in his speech to the Reichstag.

March 15: Germany occupies Czechoslovakia.

August 23: Nazi Germany and the Soviet Union sign the Molotov-Ribbentrop Pact, a non-aggression agreement.

September 1: Germany invades Poland, leading to the start of World War II.

September 3: France and the United Kingdom declare war on Germany.

September 17: Soviet Union invades Eastern Poland.

November 30: Soviet Union attacks Finland in the Winter War.

1940:

April 9: Germany invades Denmark and Norway.

May 10: Germany invades France and the Low Countries.

May 26-June 4: Operation Dynamo - Evacuation of British and Allied forces from Dunkirk.

June 22: France signs an armistice with Germany.

July 10-October 31: Battle of Britain - German Luftwaffe attacks British cities and airfields.

October 28: Italy invades Greece.

November 10: Hungary and Romania join the Axis powers.

1941:

June 22: Germany launches Operation Barbarossa, invading the Soviet Union.

December 7: Japan attacks Pearl Harbor, bringing the United States into the war.

December 8: United States and United Kingdom declare war on Japan.

December 11: Germany and Italy declare war on the United States.

1942:

February 19: President Franklin D. Roosevelt signs Executive Order 9066, authorizing internment of Japanese-Americans.

April 9: United States and Filipino forces surrender in Bataan, Philippines.

June 4-7: Battle of Midway - A decisive victory for the United States in the Pacific.

August 7: Allies invade North Africa (Operation Torch).

November 19-February 2, 1943: Battle of Stalingrad - Soviet victory over German forces.

1943:

July 10: Allies invade Sicily (Operation Husky).

September 8: Italy surrenders to the Allies.

November 28: Tehran Conference - Churchill, Roosevelt, and Stalin discuss Allied strategy.

December 16: Germany launches Ardennes Offensive (Battle of the Bulge).

1944:

June 6: D-Day - Allied forces land in Normandy, France.

July 20: Failed assassination attempt on Hitler by German officers.

August 25: Liberation of Paris.

October 20: General MacArthur returns to the Philippines.

December 16: Battle of the Bulge begins.

1945:

January 27: Soviet troops liberate Auschwitz concentration camp.

February 4-11: Yalta Conference - Allied leaders discuss post-war Europe.

April 12: President Roosevelt dies; Harry Truman becomes U.S. president.

April 30: Adolf Hitler commits suicide in his bunker.

May 8: Victory in Europe (VE) Day - Germany surrenders unconditionally.

July 16: First successful test of an atomic bomb (Trinity test).

August 6 and 9: United States drops atomic bombs on Hiroshima and Nagasaki.

August 15: Japan announces surrender.

September 2: Japan formally surrenders aboard the USS Missouri, ending World War II.